Grandaddy and Janetta Together

Grandaddy and Janetta Together

THE THREE STORIES IN ONE BOOK

By Helen V. Griffith

Pictures by James Stevenson

Greenwillow Books

An Imprint of HarperCollins*Publishers*

Grandaddy and Janetta Together: The Three Stories in One Book
Text copyright © 1987, 1993, 1995 by Helen V. Griffith
Illustrations copyright © 1987, 1993, 1995 by James Stevenson
All rights reserved. Printed in the United States of America.
www.harperchildrens.com

These stories, with text by Helen V. Griffith and full-color illustrations by James Stevenson,
were first published by Greenwillow Books in *Grandaddy's Place* (1987),
Grandaddy and Janetta (1993), and *Grandaddy's Stars* (1995).
New one-volume edition, *Grandaddy and Janetta Together*, published by
Greenwillow Books, an imprint of HarperCollins Publishers, in 2001.

The illustrations were originally created as full-color art and were converted to
black and white for this edition. The text of this book is set in Adobe Perpetua.

Library of Congress Cataloging-in-Publication Data
Griffith, Helen V.
Grandaddy and Janetta together: the three stories in one book /
by Helen V. Griffith; pictures by James Stevenson.
p. cm.
"Greenwillow Books."
Contents: Grandaddy's place—Grandaddy and Janetta—Grandaddy's stars.
ISBN 0-06-029148-6 (trade).   ISBN 0-06-029238-5 (lib. bdg.)   [1. Grandfathers—Fiction.
2. Farm life—Fiction. 3. City and town life—Fiction.]   I. Stevenson, James, (date) ill.
II. Title.   PZ7.G8823 Gq 2001   [E]—dc21   99-098197

1 2 3 4 5 6 7 8 9 10   First Edition

For Hope and Buddy

CONTENTS

PART ONE
Grandaddy's Place

PART ONE

Grandaddy's Place

GRANDADDY'S PLACE

One day Momma said to Janetta, "It's time you knew your grandaddy."

Momma and Janetta went to the railroad station and got on a train. Janetta had never ridden on a train before. It was a long ride, but she liked it. She liked hearing about Momma's growing-up days as they rode along. She didn't even mind sitting up all night.

But when they got to Grandaddy's place, Janetta didn't like it at all.

The house was old and small. The yard was mostly bare red dirt. There was a broken-down shed and a broken-down fence.

"I don't want to stay here," said Janetta.

Momma said, "This is where I grew up."

An old man came out onto the porch.

"Say hello to your grandaddy," Momma said. Janetta was too shy to say hello. "You hear me, Janetta?" Momma asked.

"Let her be," said Grandaddy.

So Momma just said, "Stay out here and play while I visit with your grandaddy."

They left Janetta standing on the porch. She didn't know what to do. She had never been in the

country before. She thought she might sit on the porch, but there was a mean-looking cat on the only chair. She thought she might sit on the steps, but there was a wasps' nest up under the roof. The wasps looked meaner than the cat. Some chickens were taking a dust-bath in the yard. When Janetta came near, they made mean sounds at her.

Janetta walked away. She watched the ground for bugs and snakes. All at once a giant animal came out of the broken-down shed. It came straight toward Janetta, and it was moving fast. Janetta turned and ran. She ran past the chickens and the wasps' nest and the mean-looking cat.

She ran into the house.

"There's a giant animal out there," she said.

Grandaddy looked surprised. "First I knew of it," he said.

"It has long legs and long ears and a real long nose," said Janetta.

Momma laughed. "Sounds like the mule," she said.

"Could be," said Grandaddy. "That mule's a tall mule."

"It chased me," said Janetta.

"It won't hurt you," Momma said. "Go back outside and make friends."

But Janetta wouldn't go back outside. "Nothing out there likes me," she said.

GRANDADDY'S STORY

After dark Momma and Grandaddy and Janetta sat out on the steps. The mean-looking cat wasn't anywhere around. Janetta hoped the wasps were asleep. She was beginning to feel sleepy herself. Then a terrible sound from the woods brought her wide awake.

"Was that the mule?" she asked.

"That was just an old hoot owl singing his song," said Grandaddy.

"It didn't sound like singing to me," said Janetta.

"If you were an owl, you'd be tapping your feet," said Grandaddy.

They sat and listened to the owl, and then Grandaddy said, "It was just this kind of night when the star fell into the yard."

"What star?" asked Janetta.

"Now, Daddy," said Momma.

"It's a fact," said Grandaddy. "It landed with a thump, and it looked all around, and it said, 'Where am I?' "

"You mean stars speak English?" asked Janetta.

"I guess they do," said Grandaddy, "because English is all I know, and I understood that star just fine."

"What did you say to the star?" asked Janetta.

Grandaddy said, "I told that star, 'You're in the United States of America,' and the star said, 'No, I mean what planet is this?' and I said, 'This is the planet Earth.' "

"Stop talking foolishness to that child," Momma said.

"What did the star say?" asked Janetta.

"The star said it didn't want to be on the planet

Earth," said Grandaddy. "It said it wanted to get back up in the sky where it came from."

"So what did you do, Grandaddy?" Janetta asked.

"Nothing," said Grandaddy, "because just then the star saw my old mule."

"Was the star scared?" Janetta asked.

"Not a bit," said Grandaddy. "The star said, 'Can that mule jump?' and I said, 'Fair, for a mule,' and the star said, 'Good enough.' Then the star hopped up on the mule's back and said, 'Jump.' "

Momma said, "Now, you just stop that talk."

"Don't stop, Grandaddy," said Janetta.

"Well," Grandaddy said, "the mule jumped, and

when they were high enough up, the star hopped off and the mule came back down again."

"Was the mule all right?" asked Janetta.

"It was thoughtful for a few days, that's all," said Grandaddy.

Janetta stared up at the sky. "Which star was it, Grandaddy?" she asked.

"Now, Janetta," Momma said, "you know that's a made-up story."

Grandaddy looked up at the stars. "I used to know," he said, "but I'm not sure anymore."

"I bet the mule remembers," Janetta said.

"It very likely does," said Grandaddy.

From somewhere in the bushes some cats began to yowl. "That's just the worst sound I know," Momma said. "Janetta, chase those cats."

"They're just singing their songs," said Grandaddy.

"That's right, Momma," said Janetta. "If you were a cat, you'd be tapping your feet."

Momma laughed and shook her head. "One of you is as bad as the other," she said.

FISH-TALK

The next day Grandaddy and Janetta went fishing. Janetta had never been fishing before. She didn't like it when Grandaddy put a worm on the hook.

"Doesn't that hurt him?" she asked.

"I'll ask him," said Grandaddy. He held the worm up in front of his face. "Worm, how do you feel about this hook?" he asked. He held the worm up to his ear and listened. Then he said to Janetta, "It's all right. That worm says there's nothing he'd rather do than fish."

"I want to hear him say that," Janetta said. She

took the worm and held it up to her ear. "He's not saying anything," she said.

"That worm is shy," said Grandaddy. "But I know he just can't wait to go fishing." Grandaddy threw the line into the water. It wasn't long before he caught a fish. Then he gave Janetta the pole so that she could try. She threw the line in, and before long she had a fish, too. It was just a little fish. Janetta looked at it lying on the bank. It was moving its fins and opening and closing its mouth.

"I think it's trying to talk," Janetta said.

"It may be, at that," said Grandaddy. He held the fish up to his ear. "It says, 'Cook me with plenty of cornmeal,' " said Grandaddy.

"I want to hear it say that," said Janetta.

"Can you understand fish-talk?" asked Grandaddy.

"I don't know," said Janetta.

"Well, all that fish can talk is fish-talk," said Grandaddy.

Janetta held the fish up to her ear and listened. "It says, 'Throw me back,' " Janetta said.

Grandaddy looked surprised. "Is that a fact?" he asked.

"Clear as anything," said Janetta.

"Well, then I guess you'd better throw it back," said Grandaddy.

Janetta dropped the little fish into the water and watched it swim away. Grandaddy threw the line back in and began to fish again. "I never saw anybody learn fish-talk so fast," he said.

"I'm going to learn worm-talk next," said Janetta.

NAMING
THE MULE

When they had enough fish for supper, Janetta and Grandaddy walked on home. The mean-looking cat came running to meet them. He purred loud purrs and rubbed against their legs.

"I didn't know that cat was friendly," Janetta said.

"He's friendly when you've been fishing," said Grandaddy.

The mule came out of the shed and walked toward them with its ears straight up. Janetta didn't know whether to run or not. The mule walked up to her and pushed her with its nose. Janetta was sorry she hadn't run.

"What do you know," Grandaddy said. "That old mule likes you."

"How can you tell?" Janetta asked.

"It only pushes you that way if it likes you," said Grandaddy.

"Really?" asked Janetta.

"It's a fact," said Grandaddy. "Up until now that mule has only pushed me and the cat and one of the chickens."

Janetta was glad she hadn't run. She reached out her hand and touched the mule's nose. "Grandaddy," she said, "what's the mule's name?"

"Never needed one," said Grandaddy. "It's the only mule around."

"Can I name it?" asked Janetta.

"You surely can," said Grandaddy.

Janetta thought. "I could call it Nosey," she said.

"That would suit that mule fine," said Grandaddy.

Janetta thought some more. "Maybe I'll call it Beauty," she said.

"That's a name I never would have thought of," said Grandaddy.

The mule gave Janetta another push. "This mule really likes me," Janetta said. "It must know I'm going to give it a name."

"You don't have to give it anything," said Grandaddy. "That mule just likes you for your own self."

JANETTA'S PLACE

After supper Grandaddy and Momma and Janetta sat out on the steps and watched the night come on. The stars began to show themselves, one by one.

"Now I know what I'll name that mule," Janetta said. "I'll call it Star."

"Should have thought of that myself," said Grandaddy.

"Tomorrow I'll give the cat a name," said Janetta.

"Only fair, now the mule has one," said Grandaddy.

"After I get to know the chickens, I'll name

them, too," said Janetta. "Then you'll be able to call them when you want them."

"That'll be handy," said Grandaddy.

"You'll be naming the hoot owl next," Momma said.

"I've been thinking about it," said Janetta.

Momma laughed, and Grandaddy did, too.

"Now, how did we get along around here before you came?" he asked.

"I've been wondering that, too, Grandaddy," said Janetta.

PART TWO

Grandaddy and Janetta

TRAIN RIDE

Momma put Janetta on the train in Baltimore.

"Be sure you mind your grandaddy," she called after her.

But Janetta was too excited to listen. She found her seat and grinned out the window at Momma. They waved until the train started. Then they blew kisses until they couldn't see each other anymore. Janetta leaned back against her seat and watched Baltimore rush past the window.

The conductor came for her ticket. "So you're going all the way to Georgia," he said.

"I'm going to visit my grandaddy," said Janetta.

The conductor smiled down at her. "Well, your grandaddy's got a treat coming," he said. He took her ticket and put her bag on the overhead rack.

At first it was fun to sit watching buildings and highways and rivers flash by. Then Janetta started to feel an empty feeling inside herself. She opened the snack bag Momma had given her and ate half a jelly sandwich and three cookies. After that she felt full and empty at the same time. She began to wonder what Momma was doing. I bet she misses me, Janetta thought. She felt so sorry for Momma that tears came to her eyes and ran right down her face.

The conductor saw the tears. "Are you sick, little girl?" he asked.

"No," Janetta said. "I'm thinking how lonely my momma is."

"Where's your momma?" the conductor asked.

"She's home," Janetta said, "and she's never been away from me before."

"I don't think your momma's lonely," the

conductor said. "She's too busy thinking about what a good time you and your grandaddy are going to have together."

Janetta's lip quivered. "It's been a whole year since I saw my grandaddy," she said. "I don't even remember what he looks like."

"A year's no time," the conductor said. "Once when I was a boy I didn't see my grandaddy for five years. But when I finally saw him, I knew him right away."

Janetta sniffed. "Right away?" she asked.

"Even though he had gone bald in the meantime," said the conductor.

"Grandaddy's bald already," Janetta said.

"Then you've got nothing to worry about," said the conductor.

"But maybe he's grown a beard," Janetta said.

The conductor laughed. "You'll know him," he said. "But even if you didn't, he would know you."

"I'm a lot bigger than I was last year," said Janetta, "and my hair is longer."

"In the five years that I didn't see my grandaddy," the conductor said, "I grew ten inches and gained twenty pounds and grew my hair down to my shoulders. But my grandaddy knew me."

"He did?" Janetta asked.

"He sure did," the conductor said. "He walked right up to me and looked me in the eye and said, 'You need a haircut.' And I looked right back and said, 'Well, you don't.'"

He and Janetta both laughed, and Janetta noticed that the empty feeling had gone away. A sleepy feeling had taken its place.

"Pleasant dreams," the conductor said. "We'll be in Georgia before you know it."

BACK AGAIN

When they got to Georgia, Janetta grabbed her bag and hopped off the train, and there was Grandaddy. Janetta knew him right away.

"Grandaddy," she said, "you don't have a beard."

Grandaddy felt his chin. "Don't recall I ever did," he said.

"I was afraid you would have a beard, and I wouldn't recognize you," Janetta told him.

"That's funny," Grandaddy said. "I worried about the same thing. I thought to myself, If that child has grown a beard, how will I ever know her? I'll have to walk up to every bearded child that gets off the train and say, 'Are you Janetta?' until I find the right one."

"Grandaddy!" Janetta laughed. "Children don't have beards."

Grandaddy shook his head. "All that worrying for nothing," he said. He took Janetta's bag, and they walked alongside the tracks until they came to Grandaddy's place.

Janetta looked around carefully to make sure nothing had changed. The house was still old and small, and the yard was still mostly bare red dirt. The broken-down shed was still there, and so was the mule. It came running across the yard, heading straight for Janetta.

Janetta wasn't scared at all, even when the mule pushed against her with its big soft nose.

"Hello, Star," said Janetta.

"He remembers that you named him," Grandaddy said. "He's proud of that name."

Some chickens were pecking in the dirt.

"Grandaddy," Janetta asked, "are they the same chickens as last year?"

"Well, the eggs taste the same," said Grandaddy.

Then Janetta noticed that something was missing. "Where's the cat?" she asked.

"Around here someplace," said Grandaddy.

Janetta called, "Here, kitty, kitty." She waited for the cat to come running, but it didn't.

"Do you think the cat has forgotten me?" she asked.

"Nothing here has forgotten you," said Grandaddy.

Janetta was glad of that. But where is the cat? she wondered to herself.

GRANDADDY'S TRIP

It was raining. Janetta sat at the table by the window and watched puddles form in the bare red dirt. The mule looked out of the shed door, shook its head, and went back inside. The chickens perched on the porch rail with their feathers fluffed out and their eyes half shut. There was no sign of the cat.

Grandaddy put an old checkerboard and checkers on the table. "This was your momma's," he said.

Janetta hadn't played checkers in a long while

but she remembered how, so they started to play.

After a while, Grandaddy said, "It was raining like this the day the mule and I planned our trip."

Janetta looked up. "What trip?" she asked.

"The mule got it into its head that it wanted to see the whole United States of America," Grandaddy said.

"How could you tell it wanted that?" Janetta asked.

"Me and that mule are close," said Grandaddy. "So I took a map out to the shed and we looked it over, and the next day off we went."

"Walking?" Janetta asked.

"Well, the mule walked and I rode," said Grandaddy. "We left at sunup and we got home just at dark."

"The same day?" Janetta asked.

"The mule is fast," Grandaddy explained, "and not much interested in sightseeing."

"Grandaddy," Janetta said, "you can't see the whole United States in one day."

"We did, though," Grandaddy said proudly. "All forty-eight of them."

"Grandaddy," Janetta said, "there are fifty states."

Grandaddy opened his eyes wide. "You don't say so!" he said.

"I learned it in school," said Janetta.

"Well, don't tell the mule," Grandaddy said. "It thinks it saw them all."

Janetta and Grandaddy went back to their game.

After a while Janetta said, "Grandaddy, if you and the mule ever go to visit the states you missed, I want to come along."

"Wouldn't go without you," said Grandaddy. "And neither would the mule."

MOUTH ORGAN
MUSIC

At night Grandaddy and Janetta sat out on the steps and watched the day finish up. As the sky darkened and the stars appeared, the air became full of sound. There were clicks and rattles and clacks and sweet high trills.

"What a racket," Janetta said.

"That's music," said Grandaddy. "Listen."

Janetta listened. She heard *treep, treep.*

"Cricket," said Grandaddy.

Janetta heard *bre-e-e-e.*

"Tree frog," said Grandaddy.

Janetta heard *katydid, katydid*.

"Katydid saying its name," said Grandaddy. "Katydid looks just like a flying leaf."

"I'd like to see that," Janetta said.

Grandaddy and Janetta sat and listened to the music.

After a while Grandaddy said, "It's my turn now." He pulled his mouth organ out of his pocket and blew into it, sliding it back and forth across his lips.

The sounds around them stopped.

"They're listening," Grandaddy said. He began to play an old-time song. "You can sing it if you know the words," he said to Janetta.

"Do the insects sing along?" Janetta asked.

"They dance," said Grandaddy. "They're down there now, dancing in the grass."

Grandaddy went back to playing his mouth organ.

Janetta looked down into a little patch of grass.

She couldn't see any insects dancing or any tree frogs, either.

Suddenly a green leaf flew up and landed on the step.

"Katydid," said Grandaddy, between notes.

The katydid flew off the step and vanished in the dark.

"Katydid invites you to dance," said Grandaddy.

Janetta was glad for the invitation, because the music did make her feel like dancing. "But I don't want to step on your friends," she said.

"You won't," said Grandaddy. "They're quick."

So Janetta jumped down to the ground and began dancing to the mouth organ music. She hopped and wiggled and spun around until she was out of breath. Then she sat back down on the step beside Grandaddy. "I didn't know I was such a good dancer," she said.

"You're better than the bugs," said Grandaddy. He shook his mouth organ and put it back in his pocket.

"Thank you, Grandaddy," said Janetta. "You are, too."

A NEW STAR

In the morning Janetta went out to visit the mule before breakfast.

The mule was back in a corner, staring at something in the hay. Janetta went over and looked. There was the cat—and not just the cat.

Janetta ran out of the shed and into the house. "Grandaddy!" she shouted. "The cat has had kittens."

Grandaddy nodded. "They do that," he said.

"I thought it was a boy," said Janetta.

"Used to think that myself," said Grandaddy. "But the cat knew better."

Janetta ran back out to the shed. She and the mule examined the kittens. Janetta held each kitten up, and the mule snuffled it with its nose. One of the kittens had a little white, star-shaped mark on its forehead.

"Look, Star," Janetta said to the mule. "This kitten takes after you."

The mule gave it another snuffle.

Janetta put the kitten back with its mother. Then she ran to the house and sat down to breakfast with Grandaddy.

"Grandaddy," she said, "there's a kitten out there with a star on its head, and it's the mule's favorite."

"How can you tell that?" Grandaddy asked.

"It got the most snuffles," Janetta said.

"A sure sign," said Grandaddy.

Janetta sat stirring her oatmeal. "Grandaddy," she said, "what are you going to do with the kittens?"

"Haven't thought," said Grandaddy.

Janetta stirred her oatmeal round and round in

the bowl. "Grandaddy," she said, "what if somebody came here and said, 'I'm looking for kittens, and I hear you have some'?"

"I'd say, 'Help yourself,' " said Grandaddy.

"Oh," said Janetta.

"Yep," Grandaddy said. "I'd say, 'Help yourself, but you can't have the one with the star on its head, because that's my mule's favorite.' "

Janetta laughed and started in on her oatmeal. "Guess what, Grandaddy," she said. "The mule's favorite kitten is my favorite, too."

SHELLING PEAS

Grandaddy and Janetta were sitting on the steps, shelling peas. The mule was standing in the shade, switching flies off its back with its tail. Every now and then Janetta threw it a podful of peas. The chickens were pecking around in the dirt. Every now and then Janetta threw them some peas, too.

The cat led her kittens out of the shed and into the yard. The kittens got busy pouncing on insects and stalking the chickens and batting the peapods.

"Grandaddy," Janetta said, "I've been thinking about a name for my favorite kitten."

"What's it to be?" asked Grandaddy.

"Well, I'd like to call it Star," Janetta said.

"Good idea," said Grandaddy.

"But that's the mule's name, too," Janetta said. "We might get them mixed up."

Grandaddy thought about it. "It could happen," he said. "I might set out milk for Star, and it would be the mule and he'd put his big foot right in the bowl. Or I'd hitch up Star to the plow, and it would be the kitten and plowing with a kitten is slow work." Grandaddy shook his head. "No, you'd better not name it Star," he said.

"But what else can you call a kitten with a star on its head?" Janetta asked.

"It's a problem, all right," said Grandaddy.

The two of them shelled peas and thought.

"Only one thing to do," Grandaddy said finally. "Get rid of the kitten."

Janetta stopped shelling peas. "Grandaddy!" she said.

"Well, we can't have two Stars around here," said Grandaddy, "and I need the mule."

"But, Grandaddy," Janetta said, "the kitten is so little."

Grandaddy kept shelling peas.

"And it's shy," Janetta said.

Grandaddy kept on shelling peas.

"And it's used to us," Janetta said.

Grandaddy stopped shelling peas and looked at Janetta. "Think it could get used to Baltimore?" he asked.

Janetta stared at Grandaddy. Then she jumped to her feet, scattering peapods everywhere and sending the kittens running for their mother. "I know it could, Grandaddy," she said.

"That's that, then," said Grandaddy, and he went back to shelling peas.

Janetta was so happy that she threw a big handful of peas to the mule. Then she threw peas to the chickens. She threw some peas to the kittens, too.

"Did I mention these peas were for supper?" Grandaddy asked.

Janetta giggled and sat back down beside him.

"That's a good idea, Grandaddy," she said, "for me to take the kitten home."

"It came to me just like that," said Grandaddy.

"Now I'll have a Star, and you'll have a Star," Janetta said.

"Sure enough," said Grandaddy.

"And Momma will have the kitten for company while I'm away," Janetta said, "so I can come to see you twice as often."

"Now that," said Grandaddy, "is the best idea yet." He dropped the last of the peas into the pot and threw the pods out for the chickens to fight over.

Then Grandaddy and Janetta went inside to cook what was left of the peas for supper.

PART THREE

Grandaddy's Stars

COMPANY'S
COMING

"Company's coming," Momma said.

Janetta stopped playing with Star and looked up. "Who?" she asked.

Momma smiled and said, "Somebody from Georgia."

Janetta stared at Momma. Star patted Janetta's knee to make her play some more, but Janetta just kept staring at Momma. "Grandaddy lives in Georgia," she said.

"I know he does," said Momma.

"But he doesn't travel much," Janetta said.

"Not a whole lot," Momma agreed.

"It's hard for him to get away," Janetta said, "because he has a mule to take care of."

Momma nodded. "He does have a mule."

"Then there's the chickens," Janetta said, "and the cat."

"That cat can take care of herself," Momma said, "and he found somebody to tend the livestock."

Janetta jumped up and threw herself on her mother. "It *is* Grandaddy!" she yelled.

Star scooted under the couch, and Momma laughed. "He'll be here tomorrow," she said. "And what are you trying to do, break every rib I've got?"

JANETTA'S LIST

Janetta lay in bed and thought about what fun tomorrow would be.

"You'll have fun, too," she told Star. "You haven't seen Grandaddy since you were a little kitten."

Janetta wondered if Grandaddy was excited about the visit. Maybe he's too excited to sleep, she thought. Then he'll fall asleep when it's time to get up. Then he'll miss the train.

Janetta jumped out of bed. She ran into Momma's room and shook her awake. "I'm worried," she said.

Momma hid her face in her pillow. "I knew I shouldn't have told you ahead," she said.

Janetta shook Momma again. "I'm afraid Grandaddy won't be able to sleep, and he'll miss the train," she said.

"If he can't sleep, he'll be early for the train," Momma told her.

"But what if he's so tired on the train, he sleeps right through Baltimore?" Janetta asked. "What if he doesn't wake up until Philadelphia?"

"He'll like Philadelphia," Momma said. "He can visit the Liberty Bell."

Janetta was pretty sure Momma was teasing, but she couldn't help starting to cry.

Momma rolled over and turned on the light. "The last thing in the world that Grandaddy would do is miss that train," she said.

As soon as Momma was good and awake, Janetta felt better. "I wrote down all my plans for Grandaddy's visit," she said. "I'm going to show him everything in Baltimore."

Janetta ran to her bedroom and got her list. Then she ran back and jumped into bed with Momma. Momma took the paper and looked at it. It said:

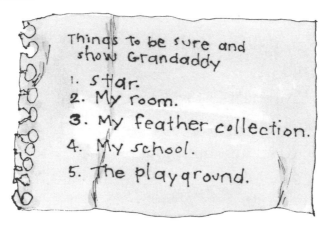

Things to be sure and show Grandaddy
1. Star.
2. My room.
3. My feather collection.
4. My school.
5. The playground.

Momma said, "Is this all you can think of in Baltimore to show Grandaddy?"

"I just wrote down the most important things," Janetta said.

Momma put down the list and turned off the light. She lay back and shut her eyes.

"Momma," Janetta said.

"Now what?" Momma said.

"I was just thinking," Janetta said. "What if the mule gets sick?"

"It won't get sick," Momma said.

"Well, what if it just pretends to be sick so Grandaddy won't leave?" Janetta said.

Momma turned her head and looked at Janetta. "Is it a tricky mule?" she asked.

Janetta thought about the mule. "No, it's not tricky," she decided.

"Well, then," Momma said, closing her eyes.

Janetta lay still for a few minutes. Then she said, "Momma."

"What now?" Momma said with her eyes closed.

"What if Grandaddy gets here, and he doesn't like it?" Janetta said.

"You're here, aren't you?" asked Momma.

"Yes," said Janetta.

"Then Grandaddy will be just fine," Momma said.

Janetta felt a lot less worried. She was even feeling a little sleepy. Then Star jumped up on the bed, looking for somebody to play with.

"Shhh. Don't wake up Momma," Janetta whispered.

But Momma was awake. "Is this the only bed in this house?" she asked.

Janetta giggled. "The only one with anybody in it," she said.

"I don't know what kind of a night's sleep Grandaddy is having," Momma said, "but I'll bet he's doing better than we are."

GRANDADDY!

Janetta and Momma were at the railroad station waiting for Grandaddy's train.

While they waited, Janetta looked over her list of things to show Grandaddy. Last night she had thought it was a good list. Now everything on it sounded boring. Janetta started to worry. Grandaddy isn't going to like it here, she thought.

Just then they saw the train coming, and Janetta forgot about her list. When Grandaddy stepped off the train, she ran to him.

"Grandaddy!" she yelled. "You're really here!"

"Was there a doubt?" Grandaddy asked.

"She was afraid you'd oversleep and miss the train," Momma said.

"Nobody oversleeps with a yard full of chickens," Grandaddy said.

"Then she was afraid you'd sleep through your stop," Momma said.

"No chance of that," Grandaddy said. "I had to

make sure the engineer didn't make any wrong turns and get us lost."

"Trains don't get lost, Grandaddy," Janetta said.

"Not with me watching them," said Grandaddy.

"Well, let's get along home," Momma said. "Janetta has a whole list of things to show you."

That made Janetta start worrying again. Her list was boring. Grandaddy wasn't going to like it here.

GRANDADDY'S
STARS

Star was waiting for them at the door. He was at the top of Janetta's list of things to show Grandaddy.

Now Janetta thought, He's just an ordinary-looking cat. Grandaddy won't care about him.

Then Star meowed, and Grandaddy stopped and stared. "Can this handsome cat be the kitten with the same name as my mule?" he asked.

"He's not as cute as he was," Janetta said.

"What do you mean?" Grandaddy asked. "That is a fine-looking cat. That cat could win first prize in a show. He could go on the stage."

Janetta looked Star over carefully and decided

that Grandaddy was right. "But he's still just a cat," she said, "not a mule like your Star."

Grandaddy picked Star up and sat down with him on his lap. "In a way this is better than my Star," he said. "When I try to hold my Star on my lap, we just can't get comfortable."

"Grandaddy," Janetta said, "your Star is a mule. Mules are too big for laps."

Grandaddy thought for a minute. "You may have something there," he said.

"Why don't you show Grandaddy around while I fix us something to eat?" Momma said.

Janetta didn't want to show Grandaddy around. There was nothing interesting to see. At Grandaddy's place there were chickens on the porch, and from the windows you could look out at the vegetable patch and the railroad track. Here you just saw buildings.

But Momma said, "Go on," so Janetta took Grandaddy to her room, because that was next on her list.

Grandaddy stood in the doorway and looked.

He thinks it's boring, Janetta thought.

Suddenly Grandaddy said, "What do you know!" and he hurried to the window.

Janetta followed him. "What is it?" she asked.

"That's the same patch of sky I see from my room in Georgia," Grandaddy said.

Janetta looked at the sky. "How can you tell?" she asked.

"By the stars," Grandaddy said. "Those stars are my own stars. They're glad to see me, too."

Janetta looked at the stars. She couldn't tell whether they looked glad or not. "How do they know you, Grandaddy?" she asked.

"We've been looking at each other for a long time," Grandaddy said.

Janetta looked some more. She began to think that maybe the stars did look glad to see Grandaddy, at that. "They don't know me at all," she said.

"Give them a wave," Grandaddy said.

Janetta waved, and then she stared very hard into the sky. "I don't think they waved back," she said.

"They will," Grandaddy said. "You just took them by surprise."

"Is anybody hungry?" Momma called, and Janetta and Grandaddy headed for the kitchen.

"Momma," Janetta said, "did you know that Grandaddy and I have the same stars?"

"I didn't know," Momma said, "but I'm not surprised."

BALTIMORE'S
BEST PLACES

At breakfast the next morning Momma told Grandaddy, "Janetta's got plans. You're going to have a busy day."

"That'll be a change," Grandaddy said. "I haven't had a busy day since the chickens decided to fly south for the winter."

"How did that keep you busy, Grandaddy?" Janetta asked.

"Well, I didn't want them to go," Grandaddy said. "But no sooner did I grab one than another would take off."

"But Grandaddy," Janetta said, "didn't you tell them that they were already pretty far south?"

"Chickens are hard to talk to," Grandaddy said, "especially when they're stirred up. If that grasshopper hadn't come along, they'd have been gone."

Janetta laughed. "What could a little grasshopper do?" she asked.

"When the chickens saw the grasshopper, they all thought, Snack!, and their traveling plans went right out of their heads," Grandaddy told her.

"Oh, Grandaddy," Janetta said, "did they eat him?"

"They chased him all over the yard," Grandaddy said, "but he was an extra lively grasshopper."

"He got away," Janetta said happily.

Grandaddy nodded. "Last time I saw him, he was headed for the high weeds," he said. "He looked worn out, but I think he enjoyed the excitement."

"I thought you two were going sightseeing," Momma said. "Where's your list, Janetta?"

Janetta took the list out of her pocket. She took a pencil and crossed off "Star" and "My room."

"What's next?" Grandaddy asked.

Janetta read, "My school."

It was really "feather collection," but Janetta had decided to skip that.

With all those chickens around, Grandaddy sees plenty of feathers, she thought. He won't care about my collection.

But when they stood in front of her school building, it didn't seem any more interesting than the feathers.

"It's ugly," Janetta said.

"It's not ugly, just serious looking," Grandaddy said. "It looks like a place where you learn

important things. It looks like a place where future Presidents go to school."

"It's just a school for everyday people," Janetta said.

"That's hard to believe," Grandaddy said. "If I'd gone to that school, I don't doubt that I'd be President right this minute."

"Presidents have a lot to do," Janetta said.

Grandaddy nodded. "Might have to put in another phone," he said.

"Grandaddy, you couldn't stay home if you were President," Janetta said. "You'd have to go and live in the White House."

Grandaddy raised his eyebrows. "Is that the law?" he asked.

"I don't know," Janetta said, "but all the Presidents do it."

Grandaddy thought it over. "Well, I guess it would be all right for a few years," he said. "That mule likes a change now and then."

"Grandaddy," Janetta said, "I don't think the mule would like the White House."

"Why not?" Grandaddy asked. "Yard too small?"

"I think there's enough yard," Janetta said, "but there's probably not a shed."

"There must be a shed," Grandaddy said. "Where else would the chickens sleep?"

"I don't think Presidents have time for chickens," Janetta said.

"No time for chickens!" Grandaddy said. "Well, it's a good thing I didn't go to that school. It would have caused me all kinds of trouble when I got to be President."

"Grandaddy, you're kidding, aren't you?" Janetta asked.

"Half," said Grandaddy. "What's next on that list?"

Janetta didn't have to look. "The playground," she said.

But when they got to the playground, Janetta wondered why she had put it on her list. It was just a weedy empty lot with newspapers blowing around in it.

Grandaddy stood and looked at the playground. "I want to remember it so I can describe it to the mule," he said. "This is the very kind of place that mule would like."

"It's just a boring empty lot," Janetta said.

"Just right for running," Grandaddy said. "No worry about stepping on pea plants or chickens or a kitten. That mule loves to run."

"I do, too, Grandaddy," Janetta said. She ran all the way across the playground and back to Grandaddy. "It *is* just right for running," she said. "Be sure and tell the mule."

When they got home, they told Momma where they had been, and Momma said, "Baltimore is an interesting city. Tomorrow we'll do some real sightseeing."

"That'll be fine," Grandaddy said, "but I've seen the best places already."

FEATHERS

Grandaddy and Janetta were at Janetta's window, looking at the stars.

Janetta waved, and then she waited. "They still didn't wave back," she said.

"Give them time," said Grandaddy.

Janetta and the stars looked at each other a little longer, and then she said, "Grandaddy, there's one more thing on my list of things for you to see." She took a box from her bookcase and handed it to him.

He opened it and looked inside. "Feathers," he said.

"I guess you see enough feathers at home," Janetta said. She was sorry she had brought out her collection.

But Grandaddy said, "Not like these." He looked carefully at the feathers, one by one. "These feathers have traveled," he said. "These feathers have stories to tell." He took a bright black feather from the box. "This one, for instance."

"I picked it up on the playground," Janetta told him.

"Well," Grandaddy said, "this could be a feather from the very bird that almost talked my chickens into leaving home."

"Really, Grandaddy?" Janetta asked. She examined the feather. "I think it's from a starling," she said.

"It was a starling that was talking to my chickens," Grandaddy said. "They would all look over at me, and then they would whisper together."

"I didn't know birds could whisper," Janetta said.

"They can do it," Grandaddy said. "They just don't do it much." He gave the box back to Janetta. "I don't recognize anybody else," he said, "but there are a lot more stories there."

"Only I don't know what they are," Janetta said.

"What you don't know," said Grandaddy, "you make up."

Janetta took the starling feather out of the box. "This is for you, Grandaddy," she said. "If you see the starling again, you can tell her she dropped it."

"I will," Grandaddy promised. "But I'll lock up the chickens first."

JANETTA'S STARS

The day Grandaddy went home, Janetta didn't feel right all day. She didn't feel like playing, but she didn't feel like sitting still, either.

"I think I'm sick," she told Momma.

"You just miss Grandaddy," Momma said.

"What's the use of having company, if you're going to feel so bad when they leave?" Janetta asked.

"Just think about the fun you had," Momma said, so Janetta sat and thought.

"I showed Grandaddy everything on my list," she said.

"That's good," Momma said.

"He said my school looked like a President's school," Janetta said.

Momma smiled. "Why don't you prove him right?" she said.

"He thinks Star could go on the stage," Janetta said.

"That would be fine with me," Momma said.

"And Grandaddy said the mule would love the playground," Janetta said.

"No mule visitors," said Momma.

That made Janetta laugh, and laughing made her feel better. She pulled Star onto her lap and kissed his ears.

"I'm glad you're not a mule," she said, and Star seemed glad of it, too. He sat and purred while Janetta made up feather stories for him and Momma.

When bedtime came, Janetta went to her window and waved at the stars before she got into bed.

Momma came in to kiss her goodnight, and she said to Janetta, "What's that big smile all about?"

"It's about Grandaddy's stars," Janetta said, pointing toward the window. She and Momma looked out at the little lights shining in the sky. "If Grandaddy's looking at them tonight," Janetta said, "he just saw every one of them wave."

Helen V. Griffith is the author of many well-loved picture books, including *Alex and the Cat* and *How Many Candles?* Her novels for older readers include *Cougar, Dinosaur Habitat,* and *Caitlin's Holiday.* She lives in Wilmington, Delaware.

James Stevenson is the author and illustrator of many popular picture books, novels, and books of poetry. His work is read and loved by readers of all ages.